A Fight Against

BearMann

Aaron Mann

Copyright © 2019 "BearMann"

All rights are reserved. No part of this publication may be reproduced, stored in a retrieval system or transmitted in any form or by any means, electronic, mechanical, photocopying, recording or otherwise, without prior permission of the copyright owner and the publisher.

Every reasonable effort has been made to trace and acknowledge the copyright holders of any material in this book and any associated trademarks. If there are errors or omissions, we offer apologies in advance. Please notify us in writing and we will endeavor to rectify the situation for any reprints and future editions.

Acknowledgements

I would like to thank the many people who have helped me develop this book, beginning with my beloved mum who bought me a guide on how to write a book. It was most helpful, of course, but not as helpful as her firm believe that I could accomplish my goal! She has always taught me that with hard work I can achieve what I want in life to make my dreams come true.

I want to thank my father who gave me help working out tough points in the plot. He is a Managing director at Dell Computers, so he was able to give me many pointers about the technological issues in the story. That was a big help!

I want to thank my dear older sister Celina. Though she and I squabble (a lot!), we are really close, and I do look up to her for inspiration and guidance. She tried hard to give me space while I was writing, and she tried not to disturb me too much. Thanks, Celina!

I want to thank my wonderful school Caldicott, where the creative writing club helped give me inspiration to take this leap. The support of the fine teachers at the school, their patience and confidence in me helped me with this project.

I believe I am very fortunate to have so many people standing behind me. I again say thanks to each and every one of them.

Aaron Mann

TABLE OF CONTENTS

Acknowledgements iii

CHAPTER 1 1
Boy, Bear and Bird

CHAPTER 2 13
The New Technology

CHAPTER 3 23
Aaron Grows Up

CHAPTER 4 33
Celina & Keerith

CHAPTER 5 47
BearMann

CHAPTER 6 61
A New Day

CHAPTER 1

Boy, Bear and Bird

Aaron woke early Friday morning. He usually woke early; the bird song called to him. He rolled out of his bed, jumped into his jeans and T-shirt and sneakers, and then he crept out of the house, grabbing a juice box and a cereal bar on the way. It was just past dawn; maybe he could catch another glimpse of the—bear! Was it really a bear he had seen yesterday? They said there weren't any bears left any more—not around Bozeman, anyway. He had two hours before he had to be back home for his home schooling—so he could look around the trails behind his house.

He lived in a secluded canyon twenty miles from Bozeman, Montana. While his parents were busy in high-tech careers in universities and corporations—Aaron lived in rural isolation at the edge of a wilderness. Ten-year-old Aaron was home schooled—with his lessons provided on a computer, prepared by his highly-educated parents, evaluated by paid teachers and then passed (or failed—which never happened) by outside mentors. All done by computers. He had to check in a set time on his computer at his desk, complete his pre-set lessons within a set time. Then his completed assignments would be graded by unseen persons somewhere else. It was all very remote. He had no human peer companions.

There was a gardener and a housekeeper. They came, each of them, a couple of times a week. Except for them, Aaron saw few other humans. It was no wonder he was so amazed when he saw the bear on that morning.

Aaron usually walked the trails behind the house every morning. The house was at the head of a lovely canyon; a stream ran from the mountains, the house sat on the stream, and so there was often wildlife around. Squirrels, rabbits, picas, chipmunks, deer, coyote, fox and even occasional elk were common. But bear had long been considered rare, if not almost extinct in the area.

He left the house as soon after dawn as he could. The grass was still damp. He entered the forest just behind his lawn; it was cool enough, but once in the darker forest, it was even cooler. Cold. Aaron shivered. He started down the path he had been on yesterday when he thought he had seen—and then—yes! There in front of him! There it was!

A BEAR! A great, beautiful black bear. Standing on four legs in the middle of the trail. Aaron stopped. He tried to remember what he had been taught about bear encounters. Stand up straight. Make noise. Show them you're not afraid. Make noise. Gradually retreat—but Aaron looked into the eyes of the bear, and he saw something he hadn't seen in a long time—a friendly spirit. He stared hard into the dark brown bear eyes.

The two looked at each other—bear and boy. I'm not afraid, boy thought, hoping bear could understand him. I love you, boy thought. Bear stood there. Then Bear laid down. Aaron had no idea what to do! Was the bear ill? Did he need help? Aaron stood still for a moment—then, he took a few steps forward, and finally he approached the bear and knelt by his side— "Are you all right?" he whispered.

Bear growled. Bears do not speak. A low, growling sound came from the bear. But amazingly, Aaron could understand Bear. "

"I'm fine. I need your help. We—the animals of the land—we need your help."

Aaron was both astonished and pleased. "How can I help, and what can I do?" he asked?

"You must become our voice in the land of the people," said the Bear.

Aaron looked at the bear. "I am only ten years old. Can I do that?"

"You can learn," said the Bear. "By the way, I am Keerith."

"I'm Aaron," said Aaron. "I'll learn. Hello, Keerith."

"There are many of us who need help—not just bears—elk, deer, marmots, even fish and frogs, down to the birds who wake you in the morning—the sparrows, magpies, bluebirds and crows—all the wildlife of the mountains and plains depend on you—we need someone to help us keep our homes safe."

"What can I do?" asked Aaron. "I can't do anything!" he protested. "I don't know what you're talking about!"

"For now," said Keerith, "you must just come with me and learn about the ways of the wild, of the real world. Meet my friends and see nature. Then you'll learn what to do."

Keerith rose and set off down the path on four legs, ambling along slowly. Aaron followed. He soon met some of Keerith's friends—a red fox, a bluebird—and best of all, a lovely sparrow named Celina, who also spoke with Aaron.

"Good morning," tweeted Celina. "I often perch on your window sill."

"I didn't know that. Do you eat bird seed? I can put some out for you." Aaron replied.

"That would be delightful! Sunflower seeds are the nicest!" she sang.

The three friends had a pleasant hour together; then Aaron remembered he had lessons to attend to. "Oh, my, I have to get to school!" he said.

"School?" the other two asked.

"Well, really, it's my computer." he said. "I have to check into my computer and do my work at an assigned time. I'm home-schooled by computer."

The animals didn't understand, but they watched as Aaron turned and jogged back toward his house.

For the next days and months, the three were a strange set—bear, bird and boy—and if there had been anyone around to see them, they would have certainly attracted some attention. But there was no one to see them in the edge-of-the wilderness canyon where Aaron's family lived. Aaron never mentioned his new friends to his mom and dad on the rare occasions when he saw them. They were at dinner only a few times a week, working at their jobs in the city of Bozeman twenty miles away most evenings until quite late. Aaron lived a lonely, solitary existence for the most part. Except for his new animal friends.

The three of them spent time wandering in the back country. From time to time, Aaron remembered what Keerith had said on that first morning about "helping them," but he put it out of his mind—he didn't see exactly what he was supposed to do, and he concentrated instead on having fun. He watched Keerith catch a trout from the stream, and though he thanked the bear profusely, he refused to share the raw fish lunch with him. Neither did he munch on Celina's offered pine seeds; he ate his own peanut butter sandwich.

One bright day, the three of them were playing near a deep pool on the stream. Aaron was skipping rocks across the smooth surface of the water. He went looking for a few more of the flat rocks that were just right for skipping, when his foot slipped, and he went sliding down the slippery bank into the water. Aaron went in over his head, and came up, shaking his head—to find himself in the grasp of one large black bear! Keerith had jumped in right after Aaron—not knowing if Aaron could swim or how deep the water was—he feared the boy was in danger. What a sight it must have been—bear holding boy up out of the water! Aaron was sputtering, but also laughing as they both scrambled out of the pool.

Celina, meanwhile, was flapping about overhead, in an absolute tizzy, not exactly sure what had happened to cause all the splashing and sputtering and turmoil in the pool below.

By the time boy and bear had gotten themselves out on the bank, they were laughing so hard they could hardly explain what had happened to Celina. It became one of their favorite shared stories—"Remember that day I fell into the pool—" that always evoked peals of laughter from all three years after. It was one of those things. You just had to be there.

On another occasion, late in the summer, when the huckleberries were ripe, the three went off to eat the berries off the bushes in the next canyon over. It was a fairly long hike, so Aaron carried a small day pack with his lunch, a poncho in case of rain, and a water bottle. He told his parents where he was going and that he was prepared for a hike. While they were on the way back from their excursion, a great mountain thunderstorm struck.

The three found shelter under a rocky outcropping, but even so, Aaron was pretty much soaked to the skin. He snuggled close to Keerith to keep warm, and there, in the gathering darkness, he tried to decide what he should do. The trail was a muddy mess and very dangerous.

"I think we should probably stay here overnight," he said to his companions. "My parents will be worried, but I think it's too dangerous to try to walk any more today. Then first thing in the morning we can go home."

"You're right, Aaron," answered Keerith. "Get some sleep."

The three slept as much as they could. Actually, Aaron slept, quite warmly, curled up in Keerith's warm fur, while Keerith kept watch. Celina also slept with her head tucked close by, sitting on Keerith's shoulder.

At first light, they arose. As is usually the case in the forest, the trails had dried quickly, and the three moved quickly over the ridge separating the two canyons.

As they did so, Keerith said to Aaron, "Perhaps you'd better go on alone. I'll bet someone will be looking for you by now."

"You may be right. We don't want anyone bumping into you! I'll see you later!" said Aaron, and he waved and headed down the trail alone as his friend melted into the forest.

It was a good thing, for in a very few minutes a forest ranger came up the trail.

"Hey, buddy, would you be Aaron?" asked the ranger.

"I would!" said Aaron.

"Well, I'm right glad to see you!" smiled the ranger. "Are you OK?"

"I sure am. I just got stuck in the rainstorm last night, so I holed up under some rocks. Then I thought it was too late and too slippery to try to walk any more, so I just stayed put until this morning. But I'm perfectly fine," said Aaron

"Sounds like you did the smart thing," said the ranger. "I've got a radio here; I'll just let everyone know you're on the way down. You just go on home, and everything will be fine, OK?"

"Yes, sir. I hope they'll have some breakfast for me. I sure could eat something!" said Aaron.

"I'll bet they can feed you," laughed the ranger, as he pulled his radio out of its case.

Aaron laughed as well, and the two walked back down the trail toward his house.

One evening when his parents Jenn and Frank were at home, they had guests for dinner. There were several other engineers and scientists, and they were all speaking about the great new technology they were all working on. They kept clapping Frank on the back, and saying what great work he was doing, and saying between he and Jenn it was going to be a whole new world, with the new wireless tech and all. The drones would be coming along soon, too, and what then—and you just never know what would be next—

Aaron sat quietly listening, and they all just ignored him as they always did. He wondered what they were talking about. It all sounded so curious and sort of scary, too. He knew what drones were. His dad had been working on them for years. They were those pilotless airplanes. What did they do, exactly? And his mom had been doing wireless tech, too. So what was new?

Aaron sat and ate the roast beef, which was his favorite, while the grown-ups went on and on about something called 6G and faster communications. He wondered what the electromagnetic radiation they kept talking about was. Finally, he grew so bored, he just left the dinner and went to bed.

AARON MANN

CHAPTER 2

The New Technology

What was new was the development of sixth generation wireless technology. It was the fastest, most revolutionary communication medium yet available. Everyone wanted it. But it required many more cell towers than there were available. It required much new construction across the entire country. Towers had to be approved by the government. The new 6G tech was sweeping across the nation. And the drones—well, they were everywhere—delivering things, carrying things—and who knew exactly what else? They did deliver detailed images of all news events all the time...

All the while, Aaron was lost in adventures with Keerith and Celina. The hardest time for him was winter, when Keerith had to spend five or more months in hibernation in a den up in the mountains. During those bleak dark days, he depended heavily on Celina, who did not migrate, but spent the winters tucked away in the trees close to Aaron's house, eating the seeds that Aaron provided daily in the bird feeder outside his bedroom window. Many other birds also flocked to the feeder, and he became familiar with many of them. Celina was the only one who actually spoke to him, but he grew to recognize many of the others, and they knew him as well. It was the birds, the winter birds, who kept him alive during the long dark days of the winter. He thought sometimes he would have just withered away and died if he hadn't had Celina and the other winter birds while Keerith was hibernating. He almost counted the days until he could see his friend the bear again.

He worked hard on his studies. As he did, he began to realize what was going on with the development of the 6G technology, but he tried to keep it out of his mind. The possibilities were not pleasant to contemplate.

One lovely late spring day he and his two friends were playing hide-and-seek along the stream in the canyon when they heard unusual noises coming from below them. It was the sound of heavy equipment making its way up the canyon.

"What's that?" asked Celina.

"I don't know," replied Aaron.

"It sounds like an engine of some kind," said Keerith.

"I'll go see. You two stay here," said Aaron.

He was twelve at the time; he would remember the day forever. He ran toward the noises. He could see the big back-hoe tearing up some trees. It was followed by some other tractor-type machines. Aaron ran out to approach the men on the machines.

"Hey, what are you doing? Isn't this supposed to be a wilderness area? You can't do that here," he shouted at the men.

"Hey, kid, get outa the way!" the man in a yellow hard hat driving the back hoe shouted at him. "You can't stop us! We got special permits! This is for the new networks! We're puttin' in the new tower! Now get outa the way or you'll get run down!"

"You can't just come in here like this! I'll get my mom and dad to stop you! We live right down there! You can't do this!" cried Aaron at the top of his lungs.

But the man driving the big machine didn't pay any attention. He just kept driving forward. Aaron was afraid he would just drive over him, so he turned and ran back toward Keerith and Celina.

"I've got to go home. Something terrible is happening. Keerith, you'd better head for the high country. I don't know what might happen if they ran across you; you might be in real danger."

"What are they doing?" asked Keerith.

"They're going to build a cell tower right here in the middle of the forest."

"That's crazy," said Celina.

"I'm going to talk to my mom and dad and see if I can stop them, but I don't know if I can," replied Aaron.

"Well, I certainly know some good hiding places. I'll stay out of the way," said Keerith.

"Celina, you stay out of their way, too," said Aaron.

"You know I will," tweeted Celina. "I'll see you at the bird feeder later this evening."

Aaron ran back down the trail toward his house. When he arrived there, his parents weren't there. That was no surprise; it was the middle of the afternoon, and they were both at work, of course. He spent a restless afternoon trying to think of arguments against having a cell tower constructed in the middle of the wilderness behind the house. It would ruin the peace and quiet; it would disrupt the view; it wasn't right!

When his parents finally returned, Aaron was distressed but calm. He felt he was prepared to make his argument to his parents. He hoped they would listen to him, that could understand that the cell tower just didn't belong where it was being built.

"Mom, dad—I really need to talk to you," he began.

"Oh, hi, Aaron," said his mom. "Not just now, sweetie, we've got so much to do this evening; we have a conference call in less than an hour with the people in San Francisco—can we chat later tonight?"

"No, mom, this is really important, I need to talk to you now," Aaron said, speaking a bit too rapidly.

"Wait a minute, son," said his dad. "Whatever is on your mind will have to wait. We've got important business. That's got to come first. You know how that is!"

"I know how it is! I know how it always is! I know how I never come first around here! Why can't you ever listen to me! Ever!" Aaron was practically shouting.

"Now wait just a darned minute, boy. You don't go shouting at your father like that!" said Aaron's mother firmly, shaking her finger at him. "If you don't want to be sent to your room immediately, you will apologize right now!"

Aaron knew he was getting nowhere, but he was losing his temper, and all the long days of being left alone and to his own devices had just gotten to be too much.

"Apologize! You've got to be kidding! I'm not going to apologize for asking to be heard! You never listen to me! You never ask me what I'm doing! I have no friends except for the ones I've made in the forest—and now your stupid cell towers put them in danger! I'm not apologizing! Not now! Not ever! Don't worry—You don't have to send me to my room—I'm going there by myself! It's the only place in this house where I feel welcome anyway!"

With that, Aaron turned his back and left the room. He slammed the door to his room and threw himself on his bed, crying childish tears. After a few minutes, he pulled himself up.

"Good grief, how stupid that was," he said to himself. "I've lost any chance to get them to stop the tower." But had he? What could he do? He crept out of the room. He heard his parents, now deeply involved in the conference call they had mentioned. He decided he would try again to talk to them once the call was over. When he heard them end the call, he went back into the study where they were seated.

"Mom, dad," he began, with his head down.

"Aaron," said his dad, voice low.

"Dad, I can't really apologize. I do sometimes feel neglected. But I have something else I want to talk about. Not that."

"Not that?" Aaron's father said with a raised eyebrow.

"Not that at all," replied Aaron.

"What is it, then?" asked his mother.

"It's the cell tower being built in the wilderness up the canyon," replied Aaron.

"Oh, my heavens," said Aaron's mother with a shaky laugh. "I thought it was something serious!"

"It is serious!" objected Aaron.

"What could be serious about the cell tower? That's just one of the many new towers that are being built everywhere. That one will be our tower—it will bring us the new 6G service! It'll be great!" said Aaron's dad.

"No, it won't. And it's destroying the habitat of many of the animals that live up there. It's damaging part of the stream bed. That's wilderness, dad. It's not supposed to be disturbed. Why are we up there, anyway?" asked Aaron.

"Well, son, the surveys found that that site was the best possible one for the location of the tower. So we got special clearance for the construction. There are quite a few of these special clearances. These new towers are going in all over the country. The new communication system will really be great; you'll see. Everyone will benefit," said Aaron's mom.

"Not everyone," Aaron argued. "The animals, the birds, they won't benefit. Their homes are being torn up. The stream is being hurt. This just isn't good for them. You've got to stop that tower. Move it. Move it right away, before any more trees are torn down."

His parents looked at him like they though he was from another planet.

"What are you thinking, boy? You know that can't be done. It's all part of the bigger plan. We can't just move one tower. It's a grid. The overall plan calls for the towers to be built a certain way. Now, don't worry about it. A few animals aren't going to make that big a difference anyway," said his dad.

A few animals. Aaron turned pale at the words. A few animals. The images of Keerith and Celina were clear in his head. And the others—the deer, the elk, the raccoons, the picas, the field mice and chipmunks—the trout and frogs in the streams—all the countless species of the wildlands in the mountains that loomed behind his house—a few animals aren't going to make that big a difference anyway.

He felt a great sickness come over him. What had Keerith asked him? "Be the voice of the animals in the land of the people"? He had failed. Miserably. What could he do? What more could he do?

Weary and worn out, he turned to leave the room.

"Aaron, we'll have dinner in half an hour," his mom called after him.

"I'm not hungry," he answered dully as he entered his room. What could he tell Keerith and Celina? He had no answers.

When he went back into the forest the next day, he sought out Keerith and gave him the bad news. The cell tower would be built. There was no stopping it. It rose like some kind of bad omen, tall and ugly, looming above the tallest fir trees in the forest. After a few long weeks of noisy and disruptive construction, the big machines left the forest, and just the tower remained, emitting a strange humming noise—and something else the animals could neither feel nor detect that was far deadlier.

CHAPTER 3

Aaron Grows Up

The years passed, and Aaron wasn't a child any more. His home schooling had progressed to the point where he had graduated from high school, and he now had a much better grasp of all that wireless technology stuff; he knew that what his parents were doing was highly sophisticated engineering communication and technological development. The drones his dad developed had many uses, both civil and military. Aaron still had his animal friends; now he better understood why Keerith thought he needed help to survive. The world beyond the forest may not be such a friendly place. Aaron still had no human friends, but he had begun to see the human world as less desirable than the world he shared with Keerith and Celina.

As part of the new wireless technology that his mother had developed, a huge number of new cell towers were being erected all over the United States, including the one near Aaron's home. Six-hundred-thousand new towers had been approved across the US. One afternoon, Aaron went into his parent's study in search of a roll of tape; he stumbled across an open page of a study about the effects of the electromagnetic radiation being emitted from the cell towers. Fascinated, Aaron began to read the study—fascinated—then horrified. He found that the effects would reduce the numbers of bees in the vicinity of the towers; that house sparrows would die as a result of the radiation; skulls of chickens will become thin; egg shells of all birds will thin. In addition, the drones his father was so proud of were causing countless issues with bird migrations and other animal behaviors. The picture painted was brutal and ugly.

When his parents returned that evening, Aaron confronted them with what he had read. They calmly replied that all of these things had been taken into account statistically; cost/benefit analysis had been applied. There will be some costs, to be sure, but greater benefits will be gained. It had all been analyzed. He was not to worry. The sum total of the result would be greater than any costs incurred. The evaluations had been done. Not to worry.

He stared at them. Birds will be misguided by the microwaves. The radiation will affect many other animals. He noted that the impact on bears in particular could be devastating. It could cause extinction. There was nothing good about any of the stuff they were doing. The world could do without a little bit faster cell phone service, he argued! The animals couldn't do without safe migration patterns or reasonable food safety.

His parents took no notice of his protests. Instead, they told him to get busy with his college applications. It was time, they told him, for him to think about his future, and stop wandering around in the forest all day. Who did he think he was, Robin Hood? Peter Pan? Get busy!

Aaron did get busy.

The very next day he went to Bozeman and went to the campus of the university there. Though he had been there a few times for concerts or other activities, he was not very familiar with it. He had always heard that university students were likely to be concerned about environmental issues, so he thought it would be a good place to start.

He found the student center. There was a sort of cafeteria place; students were seated around tables, drinking coffee and soft drinks, reading papers and books. It looked a good place to start. But he had no idea how to begin. He wanted to start a revolution, and he didn't even know how to start a conversation.

Then a young woman approached him.

"Looking for someone?" she asked.

"Yeah," he answered. "My courage. I don't know where I left it."

She looked at him with a raised eyebrow. "You been out in the sun too long, boy? Or had too much smoke?"

"Huh?" he looked down at her. "I don't know what you mean. No, I just don't know how to do what I came here to do."

"And what's that?" she asked, still obviously amused by this interloper.

"I came to start a protest. And I haven't a clue how to do that," he said, still clearly confused.

Shaking her head, she was really amused— "A Montana campus is hardly the place for protest. Go to California, country boy! Whatever do you want to protest, anyway? The high cost of legal marijuana? The driving age? Come on!"

He looked at her. "6G—the cell towers. The way the new communication system is going to kill wildlife. How harmful the electromagnetic radiation is for all the wildlife on the planet."

She stopped smiling. "You're serious."

"You bet I am. And I know this because I'm something of an insider. My parents helped invent most of it. And I'm terrified," Aaron said in a low, tense voice.

The young woman had now become serious as well.

"You want to protest?" she said.

"Yeah, I want to protest. I want to carry signs or something. People should know that the animals are in danger," he almost whispered.

"Are people in danger?" she asked breathlessly.

He looked at her. "Well, no—there's no danger to humans—the danger is almost completely limited to animals—first and worst to bees—then next to birds, whose navigation systems are badly disrupted—and then to the larger mammals—bears and others who hibernate—they will become depressed and die or be unable to reproduce. But there seems to be minimal effect on humans—why do you ask?"

"Well—I'm not sure—there might not be as much sympathy for your position if people are not in danger. You should know that," the girl said, frowning a little.

"You've got to be kidding. Don't you know that if the bees die, we don't eat? The crops depend on pollination!" Aaron cried in frustration.

"Oh, well," she said, with a wave of her hand, "that used to be true, but it's not really the case any more. We don't really need them any more. Our labs can take care of it now. We're pretty much independent of the animal kingdom these days. Just check it out."

Aaron stared at her. Independent of the animal kingdom. He remembered being held by Keerith in a rainstorm. He thought of the bear jumping in to save him when the bear thought he was going to drown. How could he tell these humans we would never be independent of the animal kingdom, even if we never came to know them as he did?

"I still think we need to try to save the animals from these cell towers, from the electromagnetic radiation. Isn't there anybody here who might be interested in protesting against it?" he asked.

"I doubt it. You see, the campus is really eager to get the new higher-speed networks. All the students want faster connections. What you're asking is for them to protest against what they've been asking for—just because of a few birds and animals. It ain't gonna fly," she said.

"Good grief! I thought this was an agricultural and forestry school! You're ready to sell your subjects down the road? Did mention this EMR will kill chickens? It results in thin shell for all birds?" said Aaron.

She looked at him. "It does what?"

"Every bird—including chickens—has a risk of getting thinner skulls and laying eggs with thinner shells."

"That is not a good thing," said the young woman, with her brow knitted. "I'm an animal husbandry major—planning to go into the dairy and poultry area. Not a good thing at all."

"Wanna join my protest?" asked Aaron.

"I'm beginning to give it some thought. By the way, I'm Rhia Brown," said Rhia.

"Hi. I'm Aaron Mann," said Aaron.

That's how the protest movement at Montana State got started. It wasn't much, but within a couple of weeks, there were a few hundred people, mostly students from the forestry and agriculture schools, plus some enlightened citizens of the community who were picketing in the town square or on the campus.

They tried to stop traffic, but the Bozeman police generally just routed traffic around them, so there really wasn't much disruption. They were generally just sort of benevolently ignored. The local twice-a-week newspaper didn't even dignify their efforts with a photo.

Until they disrupted the traffic going to the first football game of the season. That was too much even for Bozeman. That got Aaron, Rhia, and three other of the protestors arrested by the Bozeman police and taken to jail, where they were charged with misdemeanor charges relating to obstructing traffic.

Aaron's parents were called, and they posted his bail of $200. They were heartily annoyed. This time, Aaron's picture—and that of his parents—was prominently displayed on the front page of the local newspaper, as well as posted in the digital media that appeared instantly online. It made national news as well.

"Son of prominent scientists arrested in protest against parents project" read the headlines that appeared across the nation and even the world.

"Well, you've gone and done it, haven't you, now," said his father Frank, when they got home after returning from the jail.

"Dad, I just can't sit by and do nothing. Those towers and your drones are dangerous to the animals. I've asked you to try to reduce the danger. You won't. Now I've got to do what I can to force you to stop."

"Aaron, we've told you, the danger is minimal. What more can we say?" his mother Jenn implored.

"I guess there's nothing more to be said," Aaron replied. He went to his room.

Aaron was arrested again the following weekend for organizing a protest in downtown Bozeman at the city square. This time, only Jenn came down to bail him out. She told him Frank refused to come, saying he had enough of Aaron's "nonsense."

But Aaron was beginning to get discouraged by the response to the protests. Most people didn't pay much attention to the flyers and pamphlets they handed out when they were on the streets. It was as Rhia had predicted; once they heard that the EMR emitted by the towers had minimal effect on people—that it was animals and birds they were trying to protect—they just didn't seem to care.

Aaron wondered what was wrong with his own species. How could we be so self-centered, so narrow-minded that we could not see that our long-term survival depended on the survival of our animal mates?

CHAPTER 4

Celina & Keerith

One day, when he returned home after being given another warning by the Bozeman police, he went out the back door of his house to find some peace in the forest. Just as he entered the cool of the woods, Keerith came running toward him.

"What's wrong?" Aaron asked.

Keerith was speechless but turned and went back into the forest. Aaron followed. The two friends ran until they came upon a barbed-wire fence that had been erected around that ugly cell tower in the forest—where Aaron found Celina impaled. She had died of radiation poisoning emitted from the cell tower. This was the one closest to Aaron's home, that very one that they had fought against in the beginning.

    Aaron carefully untangled the tiny feathered body from the ugly wire. He removed his shirt and wrapped Celina in it. Then he carried her to a special place where he and Keerith had lunched many times. Keerith dragged himself along behind him. Aaron didn't know bears wept, but they do. Together, they buried the tiny bird. Keerith's huge claws tore at the soil creating a grave for his dear dead friend. Aaron gently lowered the tiny bird into the earth and covered her.

    "I didn't know what you meant that day. I do now." Aaron said "But I still don't know what to do. I have been trying. I really have." Aaron was crying, too. "I'm not ten any more, but I still can't do anything."

    Keerith didn't say anything. His grief was too great. He leaned against Aaron to show his support, but he was obviously distraught.

    Aaron finally dragged himself home. Once there, he was faced with the bird feeder he had always kept full of sunflower seeds for Celina, and he cried himself to sleep. When he awoke, he looked out his windows to see the ugly cell tower looming across the landscape to remind him of the future—bleak as it was. What could be done? He had no idea at all.

He went back to check on Keerith. There was no improvement. The bear seemed to be falling into a deep depression. Aaron tried to get him to eat. "Keerith not hungry."

"Come on, guy. You have to eat. You want to go fishing?"

"Keerith not hungry."

"What's that? You're always hungry."

"Not today. Maybe not ever again."

"Shall I find you some huckleberries?"

"Keerith not hungry."

"Well, then let's take a nap together, like we did when we were little, OK? We can cuddle up, OK?"

"OK, we can cuddle up. That might be nice."

So the two old friends, boy and bear, cuddled up—like a boy and his teddy bear—except it was the bear holding fast to the boy, who was by now a six-foot-tall man in his own right, there at the base of a fir tree in the forest, mourning the death of their dear bird-sister. Aaron knew there was nothing more he could do for Keerith than to just be with him in his sorrow.

Aaron went home later that day, after Keerith made a promise that he would eat something. Aaron tried again that night to make his parents see the evil effects the new communication system was having on the natural world. They smiled blandly and pushed college applications at him. They also said if he got arrested again they would not bail him out. He was on his own. When he went to bed, he felt a great depression creeping over him. He began to feel the same loneliness that had been such a part of his life before he had met Keerith and Celina.

"No!" he said to himself. "I won't be alone again!" But he was afraid it was going to be true. He didn't think Keerith would survive.

The next morning, he was up before dawn to find Keerith. He was practically running as he hit the path into the forest. He went deeper and deeper into the woods. He ran, then he walked. He was on the trail for more than an hour; still no Keerith. He called the bear's name time after time. He was becoming really frightened. What if

Keerith had died during the night all alone? "Keerith!" he called again.

"He's over here," a voice answered.

While he knew many of the other animals of the forest, only Keerith and Celina had ever spoken to him before. So far as he had ever known, they were the only ones with voices. Now, the fox was in the path and was speaking to him. It must be serious. Aaron looked down at the fox and followed quickly.

Well off the trail, he found Keerith near the stream. He was lying on a bed of soft moss, curled up, looking rather helpless, not like the great bear he was. His eyes were closed, but he was breathing. Aaron knelt beside him.

"Keerith?" he whispered.

Keerith opened his eyes. There was recognition in them and pain.

"Oh, Aaron. I didn't want you to see me like this. I thought I had come far enough to miss you. I thought…"

"And you would have gotten away with it if Fox hadn't given you up."

"That Fox, he's a sly one," said Keerith. "Never could trust him."

"Well, I'm glad. I wouldn't want you to be alone. I know how hard it is to be alone. You shouldn't be alone at difficult times."

"That's really nice of you, Aaron," said Keerith, with a sigh. "it makes me feel better to have you here."

"I'm glad that it makes you feel better. I want you to know that I love you Keerith. You're my brother, Keerith, and I love you," said Aaron.

Keerith looked at Aaron with his beautiful brown bear eyes and said, "I love you, too, Aaron." And then he closed his eyes.

Aaron sat there for a long while. He wasn't sure how long it was that he sat there by the side of the dead bear.

Finally, he got up to begin the long, lonely walk back toward his house. As he left the little clearing where the body of the dead Keerith lay, he saw Fox.

"Thank you, Fox," he whispered, "I owe you a great deal. I would have hated not to be able to say goodbye to him."

The fox dipped his head but said nothing. Their eyes met for a moment, and then the small red creature darted into the underbrush and disappeared.

Aaron wondered if he should try to bury Keerith. An impossibility, he decided. It would be better and more natural if he allowed the animals of the forest to make use of his friend's body for their purposes—to feed on him as they would if he had died under ordinary circumstances. That way, he would be doing some good by his death. It would be what Keerith would want, Aaron was certain.

By the time Aaron returned home, it was twilight. His parents weren't home, but Aaron didn't care. He felt completely removed from them. He felt completely removed from everything.

Aaron sat down at his computer and wrote the following letter:

To Mom & Dad,

I have asked you to stop this awful and deadly electromagnetic radiation system that you have fostered upon the animal kingdom. I have begged you to reconsider the multiplication of drones that can have such awful impact on our animal cousins. You have refused to consider my concerns. I cannot live in a world where humans refuse to take into account their animal brethren. Therefore, I am choosing to leave it.

Aaron

He sent the letter via e-mail to the accounts of both of his parents. Then he grabbed his car keys, took his small electric car, drove a few miles down the road, parked his car on the railroad track, and waited for eight o'clock high-speed freight to come flying through. It did.

The investigating officers said there was practically nothing left of the tiny car; the license plate enabled them to identify the occupant. Aaron's parents were horrified—why would he do such a thing? There must have been something wrong with the car—it couldn't have been—No way—but they hadn't read their e-mail yet.

Aaron's spirit flew from that awful wreck into the space where spirits soar—

Into a vast empty void. There was only black space. Aaron's sad, angry spirit floated around the empty space for what seemed endless time, growing more and more angry, more and more hopeless. Then a voice came to him from the emptiness of space.

"Aaron, what do you want?"

"I want what I have always wanted: to help my friends—the animals of the earth, especially Keerith and Celina. But they are gone, dead—I couldn't help them. I have failed them. I have always failed. I failed again," wailed Aaron.

"What would you do to help them?" the voice asked.

"I'd do anything!" cried Aaron. "Anything!"

"Would you join your spirit with theirs? And return to earth to do battles against the forces that are harming the animals?" asked the voice.

Aaron couldn't believe what he was hearing. "Of course, I would! I'd do anything!" he said again.

"It would be painful. And it would be most unpleasant. And you would not be human—not human at all. You must understand that," said the voice.

"I'm not human now," replied Aaron, already aware that he had no shape or form as he floated in a vast empty void without any shape of his own.

"True enough," replied the voice, a bit sarcastically. "Good of you to notice."

Aaron said, "What do I have to do?"

The Voice said, "Nothing. All in good time. It will happen."

And then it seemed the Voice went away. Aaron called out, "Where are you? Who are you? Have you gone away? What do I do now? You said I would join Keerith and Celina? What I wouldn't give to see them? But I can't see! I can only feel? And all I feel is empty! So empty!"

And then—he didn't feel so empty! He felt Keerith was with him! He felt that the bear was there, near—no, not just near—but INSIDE of him!

"Keerith! Is that you?" he whispered.

"Yes, it is, my brother," he heard in his head.

"Keerith, I've been so lonely without you," sobbed Aaron.

"And, I, without you," replied the bear, "but now we will never be apart, because we are one.'

"How can that be?" asked Aaron.

"We are going to be a spirit being, here in the spirit world, and soon, on earth as well, I understand," said Keerith.

"Will Celina be with us? The Voice said Celina will be with us," Aaron asked.

A new voice entered Aaron's consciousness. "Yes, I'm here, too," he heard Celina's familiar tweet.

"Oh, I can't believe it; we're all together!" sighed Aaron. "This all I ever wanted in life, and now I have it in death!"

"Yes, but, remember—you've promised to become an instrument to fight the evils that are rampant on the earth. That may not be so easy—or so wonderful," said Celina. In fact, it may considerably less than wonderful.

"I'm willing to take on any task. All through my like— I kept wondering what I could do. Maybe now I can figure it out. Maybe now I can do something," said Aaron.

"Maybe now WE can do something. But for the time being, we just have to wait until we get transformed into whatever earthly shape is chosen for us," said Keerith.

"I wonder what that might be," said Celina.

"I don't know," replied Keerith. "It will have to powerful to be able to fight those cell towers and drones."

Aaron wondered, too. He also wondered what he would be expected to do when his new form was developed. Would he be given a mission, or would have to come up with a plan of his own? Would he retain his own consciousness, or would he just sort of be unleashed? Everything was just a great unknown stretching before him. He was once again floating—but now, at least, he was floating in the company of the only two beings he believed had ever loved him. He was happy.

Then something began to happen. He began to sense—with human-like senses—a change coming over him. Suddenly, he realized he was no longer in a void, but in a mountain clearing. All around him were tall Douglas firs and spruce trees similar to those near his home. It appeared to be late spring; small animals were darting about. Aaron sensed that he was very tall, taller than most of the trees around him. "Strange," he thought. He looked down at his body, and he was amazed to see what looked like Keerith's body—the body of a bear!—except for his arms—in place of his arms, there were wings, but not just any wings, huge heavy wings, on the end of which were Keerith's talons!

"Good heavens! What am I" gasped Aaron.

AARON MANN

Chapter 5

BearMann

"You are BearMann!" said the Voice out of nowhere. "And you will spend the month or so working with Keerith and Celina learning how to use your new body to its fullest extent. You also have a few special additional powers; your sight is especially keen. Your sense of smell is even better than a bear's usually is. You can hear better, and because you are also a human, you can distinguish what those sounds are better than animals can. But mainly, you have massive strength and great speed. You can fly, but you need practice. You will have to figure out how and what to eat; that will take some getting used to!"

Aaron was completely astonished at all of this information. Keerith and Celina were also surprised by it, but perhaps less so.

"Once I get used to being BearMann," Aaron stumbled over the word, "what am I supposed to do?"

"I think you can figure that out on your own," said the Voice.

"Well, maybe, but couldn't you give us a clue or something?" begged Aaron.

His plea was met with silence. Apparently, the Voice had left them—BearMann alone in the forest to start figuring who—what—he/they were.

And that turned out not to be such an easy task. Having huge wings might seem to be a great thing, but if you've been used to arms your whole life, it's not so wonderful. Then it turns out that a bear prefers to walk on all fours, so the bear part of the new BearMann really wanted to do that, but the wings made that out of the question. Altogether, the newly-created creature wasn't quite comfortable with himself. Then there was the issue of eating.

Aaron consulted with Keerith. "I'm hungry, Keerith, but I'm not sure I can eat what you do, and besides, I'm not sure how I can get anything to eat with these wings," Aaron said (really he thought) to Keerith.

"I can understand the problem, Aaron—or BearMann, I guess I should say," Keerith replied with a definite chuckle in his tone-of-thought.

Celina butted in, "This is a serious problem. If he doesn't eat—we all die. Let's figure it out."

Eventually, Aaron was able to manage controlling the wings well enough so that he could knock fruits from branches and pick them up with his mouth. He learned to fish with them, though not as well as Keerith had been able to do. His incredible sense of sight and smell helped with that. Aaron was surprised at the things he enjoyed eating, now that he had a bear's body. And, of course, he was able to kill small animals, a fact that initially disturbed him greatly, but which Keerith pointed out to him was done by bears only very rarely. Bears usually ate meat only when they found it already dead. They are omnivores, like humans, eating everything available, existing mainly on vegetation and berries.

After a couple of months, BearMann was doing well in his new body. His flying was probably his weak spot. Here Celina was his tutor. Though she had been a tiny house sparrow, she understood the principles of flight, and she was able to give him pointers on managing his new wings. What he couldn't do was fly very high; he didn't want to risk discovery, and the skies were full of his father's drones, making deliveries, carrying various messages, assisting communications, and doing who knows what else. He certainly didn't want to be discovered before he began his mission of destroying them! So he had to limit his practice flights to low ones within the wilderness area.

The flights did enable him to discover what he had initially guessed. They were close to his old home. The cell tower where Celina had died was just a few miles away, and his parents' home was near it. He had chosen BearMann's first target.

The morning came in midsummer when Aaron/BearMann was ready.

"Friends, today's the day. I am going to embark on the mission of vengeance. I'm Aaron no more. I am BearMann. Let nothing stand in my way. I will begin with the cell tower that killed Celina. It comes down."

Aaron/Keerith/Celina had taken a new earthly form. Imagine a bear's body—muscled, bear face—but huge! Bird's wings—once again—huge! Those claws! On the end of those wings! Teeth! The earth shook when this being moved about. BearMann! Full of negative energy—this new being took to attacking users of technology—starting with the cell towers that were emitting the dangerous electromagnetic energy.

BearMann would appear, seemingly out of nowhere and he would rip the towers down with his bare bear hands—tossing the parts around like toys. He would pull drones out of the sky and throw them to the ground, so they could not disrupt the flights of birds. BearMann would attack technology whenever it crossed his path. BearMann became the terror of the countryside as well as the cities. He wrecked autos on the highways as they used the new communication systems. He tore antenna systems off roofs. Any sign of technology was not safe.

He attacked the offices of the corporations that were the biggest users of technology. He destroyed huge banks of computers, upsetting the nation's communication system and even the international internet. People everywhere began to call for the government to take action. They were frightened not just for their technology—but for their very safety.

BearMann had no concern for anything—not property, not human life. If it got in his way, too bad.

By the time BearMann had destroyed most of the towers in ten western states and seemed to be well on the way to doing the same in every other state in the union, the President called an urgent meeting of his Cabinet and Security Council to seek advice on what could be done. The Congress was already holding multiple committee meetings, and all the states involved were in shambles. Aaron's parents were called to the White House and asked to offer suggestions.

There were many scientists and engineers at the White House meetings, and everyone had an idea, but none seemed viable. Some suggested trying to drop a bomb on BearMann. It was pointed out that would result in mass destruction and huge civilian casualties. Using a huge military force had similar issues, and it would also probably result in the destruction of the force, given BearMann's obvious strength. Drones weren't the answer; he had knocked down everything they had sent against him.

Finally, Frank, Aaron's father suggested that he could design a monster robot, equally as large as BearMann, equip it with powerful Artificial Intelligence capable of doing battle with BearMann, and send it out to battle with him.

The problem would be to get the two to meet somewhere where there would be few or no additional casualties. They shouldn't meet in some city where they could cause massive damage to property and maybe kill hundreds of civilians as well.

The government seemed to think the plan had merit—if such a robot could be built—and if such a meeting could be managed in a place where few others would be endangered. Tough problems indeed.

Frank and Jenn were given the assignment of designing and building the robot and its AI (Artificial Intelligence). By now, they realized that Aaron had, indeed, taken his own life, and they may even have had an inkling that what was happening in the world was due in part to their refusal to listen to their son—but they refused to admit it to themselves.

They went to work in their labs—all the while, BearMann was out there, tearing down cell towers, destroying computers, incidentally occasionally killing people. Jenn and Frank designed a monster robot, smarter than anything had ever been before. As big as BearMann.

The other problem—how to get them to meet somewhere outside of a city—that was a little harder. Then Jenn had an idea.

"Why don't we announce we're going to build a new, bigger tower out in the middle of nowhere because it will be easier to protect it there? We can start construction on it, put some steel up—lure BearMann to the site that way," she said. "Once he's there—our robot can get him."

"That just might work!" answered Frank. "We could do it up here on the plains; we've got open space north of Bozeman. Nothing but wheat fields. We can buy out some farmers for a couple of months—that should work."

"Let's call the government and see what they think. I think we can set a trap this way," responded Jenn.

Of course, the government agreed with the plan. What remained was to get the robot built. That would be no small project, what with BearMann running around tearing up so many engineering facilities and computer companies, but in a few months, the huge machine was finally assembled and delivered to Montana. The acreage north of Bozeman was secured and prepared to become a construction site for a huge new cell tower.

News reports were being prepared about the new cell tower being built on the plains north of Bozeman. The reports say it will have the highest levels of electromagnetic energy yet. It will improve communication for the entire northern plains area. It will be great for the system. All of this, of course, is just to lure BearMann to the site when the fake construction begins and the huge new robot is put in place to attack him.

The robot is a shiny metallic thing, but it does have a semi-human face. That face bears a striking resemblance to Aaron. Frank had sent a photograph of his son to the maker and asked him to model the face after the photo. When Jenn saw it, she went pale.

"Good heavens, Frank, why did you do that?" she asked.

"I thought you'd like it," he answered. "I thought we'd make it kind of a monument to Aaron."

"I don't think I do," she said. "I don't think Aaron would like what we're doing."

"I don't guess he would," Frank frowned. "But it's too late now. What's done is done. I can't take it off."

"I guess not," Jenn shrugged. "But I wish you hadn't done it all the same."

"What shall we call it?" Frank asked.

"Certainly not Aaron," replied Jenn.

"How about Technoman?" said Frank.

Jenn cringed. "That's awful. With that face. That's really awful. Aaron would absolutely hate that."

"You're right. But the press will love it. And that's what counts these days. You know that," said Frank.

Jenn shook her head and turned away in disgust. She knew he was right, and she knew the robot would be called Technoman. With her son's face. She had a sick feeling in her stomach. Something was not going to be OK about all of this. Nothing had gone well since her child had –OK, admit it—committed suicide.

The days moved along, and it was midsummer. Steel girders began to move down the highway toward the site north of Bozeman. Construction tape was strung. Heavy equipment was parked in the fallow wheat fields. It started to look like something was going to happen there. A large temporary building was set up as a construction shed. One night, very late, Technoman was delivered to the building, ready for an ambush should BearMann appear on the scene. He had been programmed and was ready for any incursion by the spirit monster.

There were few humans at the site, but those who were there were equipped with recording equipment. Everyone, especially the government, wanted a record of what they believed would be an epic battle between the two strange combatants, should it in fact come to pass.

"Hey, guys, what have you heard about this monster?" one of the government agents posing as a construction worker asked another.

"I've heard he's gigantic. Supposed to look like a bear, they say," responded his friend.

"Why would a bear attack cell towers?" wondered the first man.

"I don't know. Somebody said it's a genetic freak—because of the radiation, y'know. Because of the radio waves or something," said the other worker.

"Jeez, that's kinda scary. Do ya suppose that could have any effect on us?"

"I sure hope not. I've been working around this stuff for ten years."

"Yeah, me too. That's not good news at all."

The two men hoisted their recording equipment and went into the construction shed where Technoman was housed, ready to meet BearMann when he showed up on the scene.

They waited. And they waited. In the meantime, the fake construction had to move forward—though at an agonizingly slow pace, since there was going to be no cell tower constructed at all. It just had to look like there was going to be one. Occasionally, a visitor from Bozeman or one of the other nearby towns would drop by and have to be hustled off the site—"Too dangerous around here for guests"—no one wanted anyone to catch a glimpse of Technoman reclining in the construction shed! Or to realize that there was no real construction going on at all. Or that there were far too few workers for the type of work that was supposed to be done. It was all very hush-hush. So they just waited.

The day did come. BearMann came rumbling across the plain. The earth shook. Technoman rolled out of the construction shed. The "construction workers" raced to take cover and took out their recording equipment, ready to capture the epic battle to come.

What happened was unexpected.

BearMann approached the site, ready to start smashing things as usual. Then the giant robot stepped up, looming as tall as BearMann himself. BearMann stopped dead in his tracks—stared at the robot—and lowered his wings. He continued to stare at the robot. Technoman also did not move. He was not programmed for such an event. He was waiting to be attacked. The two monster beings seemed transfixed, there on the plains of Montana.

Aaron stood there. He was looking into his own face. For the past several months, he had run on rage, pure and simple. He had suppressed all human emotion except anger; he had done nothing but eat, sleep, and destroy. He'd spent very little time communicating with Keerith and Celina; he'd just rocketed from target to target, pulling drones from the sky, tearing cell towers to the ground. Now he stood on the plains of Montana, staring at a giant robot with his own earthly face staring back at him. It him like a rock. Why would they do this?

Did they know he couldn't just attack his own image—again? That he had already killed himself once and could not do it again? His rage now dissolved into great sorrow and helplessness. How they really must hate him, to use himself against him! In his anguish, he could nothing but flee—he had failed his animal friends yet again! And he lifted himself—into the air--

"What the…?" "I never…." "What's going on?" The recording devices all captured the image of the great BearMann flying off into cloudy sky. The men there were gasping at what they had seen. They were quick to get on their phones—

The recorders were capturing this strange turn of events. Several minutes passed as the two giants just stood there. Then BearMann turned and simply flew away.

Chapter 6

A New Day

The government was quick to blame Frank and Jenn. "What kind of an attack robot is that? It didn't attack!"

"I don't know!" Frank was totally bewildered. "I don't know why it didn't attack!" He turned to Jenn, who was primarily responsible for the design of the AI, "Why didn't he attack?"

"I think I may have an idea," she said softly, "but it's a little weird. I think it's the face."

"What are talking about?" asked Frank, looking at her with narrowed eyes. "Why would the face make any difference?"

"I think that BearMann has a close connection with Aaron. And when he saw Aaron in your Technoman—he couldn't attack him—it would be kinda like attacking himself," she half-whispered.

"You've got to be kidding," Frank almost shouted. "That's absolutely crazy!"

"Yeah, and what's not crazy, these days?" she shouted back. "I didn't sign on to kill my son. I didn't sign on to be part of this whole mess. I'm getting tired of this, Frank. I may want out."

"Don't you think it's a little late for that now?" Frank roared.

"It was too late when Aaron killed himself, I suppose," Jenn cried.

"He didn't kill himself! His car stalled on the tracks!" Frank yelled.

"That's not true and you know it! You got his e-mail. You know how upset he was. He wanted us to stop. He wanted us to save the animals. I think that may be him or some part of him out there, Frank, I really do!" Jenn sobbed.

"Now you are crazy! I should have you committed!" Frank said in a low, threatening voice.

Jenn looked at him. "Do that. Maybe I'd have some peace. Maybe I could sleep." Her voice was very tired. She got up and walked out of the room.

He followed her. "So what do we do now? How do we get the robot to attack BearMann? Remove the face?"

"I don't know if that will do it. We can try changing the programming in the robot—make it attack even if it's not attacked. Right now it's only going to attack if it's approached and attacked. But we are back to square one about getting them together; I don't know how you're going to do that again," said Jenn.

"I guess that's what's next," said Frank. "I'll call the government."

Jenn spent a couple of hours re-working the programming of the AI of the Technoman robot. On a few dry runs at the North Bozeman site, the robot attacked mock targets without any provocation at all. They also removed the face from the robot, so it looked more like an anonymous machine and less like an identifiable being.

Now the only problem—luring BearMann back to the site. How could this be accomplished? No one had any ideas.

Then Jenn had one. They had all that video of BearMann flying away from Technoman without a fight. Granted, there had been no confrontation of any kind. But what if they used that video to claim that technology had defeated BearMann? After all, he had left. Couldn't one claim he had "fled"? If they handled it right, they might be able to get him to come back to the site to try again. Just maybe. It was worth a try, because they had few other chances, and BearMann was still tearing down cell towers on a regular basis, disrupting communication regularly.

So they took the video and edited it to show BearMann and Technoman approaching each other—then BearMann simply flying away. The voiceover said that BearMann was so intimidated by Technoman's obvious superiority that he decided to allow the continued construction of the giant cell tower in central Montana. That construction—currently plagued by some delays in delivery of needed materials—was scheduled to begin again soon. Technoman was at the site to continue to guard it against BearMann or anything else that might affect it. The site was critical to the development of the future of the new communication system. Altogether, the story was designed to make the site seem like the very peak of technological development—and Technoman the guardian of it. The story ran on every TV and other communication medium in the nation. It could not be missed.

BearMann did take notice of all the publicity. Aaron knew all too well what was wanted. They wanted him to come back to the site, to take on Technoman. His sorrow now matched his anger. They did, in fact, he believed, want him to kill himself yet again. They would never have enough of him until he was gone from the universe. Even his parents. He had no one but Keerith and Celina.

"Friends, I have failed you again. I can't stop the spread of the technology that is killing you. But if you agree, I can we can make one last great stand. We can go back to that cell tower construction site and fight Technoman. I don't know if we can win. But we can make a great statement against those EMR towers. If we lose, we will, all three of us, die together. But we will be together, as we have always been."

"Aaron, you were there for me when I died on earth. I will be with you always. You don't even have to ask," whispered Keerith.

"I will fly with you always," sang Celina in a soft voice.

"Then we will go to the fight as one against the evils of this awful technology that is killing the animals," sighed Aaron. "May we have the strength of all the animal kingdom on our side. We'll need it."

"You'd better get a good rest before you go. Build up your strength. Get as much on your side as you can," counseled Keerith.

"That's a good idea," said Aaron. "I am weary. I need rest. I will take a bit to get ready. I'll spend some time eating and sleeping to be in the best shape. That thing is a robot; it doesn't need anything, but I do. So let's take some time to get ready for this battle."

Aaron hid in the mountains, eating huckleberries and other autumn delicacies, building up as bears do as if he were preparing for along winter. He was preparing for a hard fight. His muscles were hard and strong; his senses were keen and sharp. He began to feel a strange sense of calm, as if he were drawing near to a major climactic event in his existence. Indeed, he was.

Once again, the site north of Bozeman waited. The only difference this time was that Technoman was not hidden. He was on constant, open patrol, with his sensors constantly searching for any sign that BearMann was approaching either on land or through the air. He walked the perimeter of the construction site night and day, his lights flashing eerily.

Civilians in the area had been asked to notify the authorities of any sighting of BearMann. Everyone was on the alert. There was a wide perimeter created around the site; no one was allowed inside the perimeter. There was an average of three false alarms a day. Usually it was somebody's cow that had strayed; once it was a bull elk bugling in the distance. Mostly it was nothing at all. The tension was high. Days went by. Nothing happened.

Then, as autumn drew toward winter, days grew shorter, tempers in Montana grew shorter along with them. Finally, it did happen. On a cold day, with temperatures hovering near freezing, the clouds hung low over the plains. Snow seemed imminent. Then, out of the low cloud bank, BearMann landed in the middle of the cell tower construction site. No sooner had he hit the ground than the newly anonymous Technoman came roaring out of the construction shed, arms raised, rushing toward him. This time, BearMann raised his wings in self-defense—but Technoman struck him—hard.

BearMann reeled from the blow, but he did not go down. The two fought fiercely around the construction site for over an hour—there were flashes of electricity, and crashes of noise, but it was impossible to tell if either party was injured in any way. Pieces of metal flew from Technoman, but he didn't seem to be diminished. Feathers flew from BearMann's wings, but he didn't slow down. He was able to fly above Technoman and beat him with his clawed hands. Neither beast was knocked to the ground. It seemed like it would go on forever.

The battle was being recorded by the onlookers from many different angles. None of them knew what would finally happen. No one would have bet on the outcome; the opponents seemed so evenly matched.

The twilight deepened, and it was getting colder and colder. Snow began to fall. The construction site was equipped with flood lights that automatically came on at twilight, and, as they popped on, they gave an eerie light to the crazy scene playing out on the bare ground of the site. Two other-worldly beings engaged in a violent battle, crashing into each other, smashing about—casting long, strange shadows against the construction shed and the empty fields. It was like something out of a nightmare

And then Technoman seemed to gain an edge. He got his arms around BearMann's neck—and BearMann, with his wings, could not bring his arms up to break the hold. Technoman appeared to whisper something in BearMann's ear—BearMann shook his head "No"—Technoman tightened his grip—Still "NO"—Tighter still—BearMann was shaking—even tighter. Finally, almost falling to his knees, BearMann appeared to agree. Technoman let him fall to the ground. BearMann slid to his knees. Technoman let out a blood-curdling noise—not exactly a yell, but a machine noise that all present would forever remember. It was a victory noise for sure. BearMann flexed his wings gingerly a few times.

It was still snowing heavily, starting to stick on the ground. Nonetheless, BearMann stood slowly and with a few tentative flaps of his wings, he took off into the cloudy sky.

"Why did he let BearMann go?"

"What is going on?"

The questions were many—the government was screaming, Frank was screaming, everyone was screaming. But the fact was—Technoman had defeated BearMann at the construction site. And three weeks had gone by and there had been no sign of BearMann anywhere. If he were still alive, and no one knew if he were, he wasn't tearing down cell towers.

Frank and Jenn sat in their study twenty miles outside of Bozeman.

"He was right. The whole 6G thing is wrong," said Jenn. "I am going to make a public statement tomorrow coming out against my own research, showing how it causes major environmental damage, not just to wildlife but to domestic animals as well. I can't live with myself anymore."

Frank stared at her. "You can't be serious. Your career will be over."

"The hell with my career. My career killed my son. Now it's killing me," sighed Jenn. "I'm done with it, if that's what it takes. I can start over, using what I know to create new form of safer energy. 6G is not worth half the wild animals on the planet. It's not worth all the song birds in the hemisphere," said Jenn with some fury in her voice, "and it surely wasn't worth my son's life."

"I don't think you can blame that on the science," Frank said in a weary voice.

"No? Well, not on the science, but certainly on our insistence that the science was more important than anything else—even what effect the implementation of that science would have on the natural world," responded Jenn. "Nobody could argue that about the splitting of the atom, could they?"

"That's a little extreme, don't you think, Jenn?" protested Frank.

"No, I don't," Jenn replied. "This could have effects almost as great. The reduction of species might be as wide spread and have as much impact as the atomic revolution. In any case, count me out. In fact, you can count me into the counter revolution. I'll be taking Aaron's place. And I have a much higher profile than he did."

"Do you know what you're saying?" asked Frank.

"Indeed, I do. I'm saying I'm ready to admit I have been wrong about what I have been doing for the past ten years; that I have failed to consider that total social and economic consequences of my research. Now that I have done so, I wish to repudiate that research. I cannot prevent others from pursuing that research, but I would strongly urge against it. I would urge the public to discontinue use of the 6G networks; they should realize that while 6G causes no immediate threat to humans, the long-range harms are devastating due to the damage to the overall environment—shall I go on?"

Frank sat there—open-mouthed. He knew what a powerful effect such words coming from an authority such as his wife would have. More than that, hearing Jenn say these words aloud was having a powerful effect on him. He knew they were true as well. He simply hadn't wanted to admit them. He also knew that equally bad things could be said about the proliferation of drones for which he had been primarily responsible. They were disrupting bird and other wildlife migrations all across the nation; most recently, a herd of antelope in Wyoming had been severely affected by a swarm of delivery drones. The animals had scattered, and it had taken days for them to re-assemble, precious lost days on their trip to winter feeding grounds. Had cost/benefit analysis taken the antelope into account, he wondered? What was the "cost" of a day lost on a migration trip for an antelope herd? Had an accountant ever even heard of such a thing? Had an accountant ever even seen an antelope? Frank had.

"Jenn, I may be willing to take another look at what we've been doing. I think this whole new grid may be getting out of hand after all," Frank said in a low voice.

Jenn looked at him intently. "Do you mean that? If the two of us—together—came out publicly against this network—we could really have an impact, you know. We really do have a big voice. Together."

"Yes, I think you're right. We might even be able to talk to the White House directly," said Frank.

"Wow, Frank, that's a great idea! I wouldn't have thought of that! Do you think we could! Let's give it a try! I can get all the info together—all the stuff on how all the damage is being done, and we can try for an appointment with the President or at least some of his people…"

"Let's get going—we've got all that stuff—we don't have any time to waste. We can get some of our friends to give us a hand if we need more data," said Frank. He was already becoming enthusiastic about opposing the 6G networks, the same systems he had been so wildly supportive of for a decade or more. The image of scattering antelope haunted him. He wouldn't mind pulling a few delivery drones out of the Wyoming sky or knocking a few cell towers off the Montana horizon after all.

It took some trying, but Frank and Jenn did get an audience with the President's Scientific Advisory Council. When they presented their case against 6G and drone expansion, it made headlines around the world.

"Major Scientists Frank & Jenn Mann Reverse Course: OPPOSE 6G!"

The reaction was swift but divided; many argued that the nation was too far along on its commitment to 6G to stop now; many of those using the system were very fond of its high speed and other advantages. But many were also shocked to learn of the many costs that would have to be paid—the loss of all song birds within just a few decades. The extinction of many common wild mammals—bears, probably most migratory species, many small ones like chipmunks. Any bees or wasps in the vicinity of any of the towers. And on and on. Then there was the drone issue—once again, disruption of migration, minor noise pollution that offended many animals (as well as people), potential privacy issues—

The debate was a national discussion. Many wondered why it taken place before the system had been started in the first place, a question that remained unanswered. Scientists lined up on both sides of the issue, some arguing in favor of the system, most seeming to argue against it.

It finally seemed to boil down to more of a moral issue than a scientific. Of course, it was possible to have the 6G system with it incredibly fast, clear and powerful transmission service, delivering voice, data, pictures and motion to everyone everywhere in the country. If we were willing to pay the cost—killing off huge numbers of wildlife, risking the pollinators of crops, imperiling much of the birdlife on the planet, destroying the beautiful vistas of many of our most lovely horizons, and the list went on.

Eventually, an unusual step was taken. There was a national referendum, a vote. The votes were recorded digitally, of course, and an astounding 83% of registered voters cast ballots. Of those voting, 85% voted against 6G, preferring instead to protect the last vestiges of the natural world against the intrusion of more and taller cell towers. The referendum also included a restriction on the number and type of civilian drones that could be licensed, effectively reducing their use.

Soon there was a major reduction in the number of cell towers across the nation. The landscape became cleaner. Yet, there wasn't much change in communication systems after all. Even those people who had 6G didn't miss it once it was gone; after all, they still had birds singing in the trees!

Frank and Jenn spend their time and energy working on ways to make existing systems more efficient. They also work to protect all species, to see life on the planet extended, not extinguished. They have created the Aaron Mann Foundation for Life, devoted to research into preservation and protection of all animal species on earth. Jenn especially thinks about Aaron daily; she wonders if there wasn't more she should have done.

Frank also soon realized that when Jenn re-programmed Technoman's AI to attack without provocation, she also adjusted his end programming—the robot didn't have to kill BearMann if he could secure from him a promise to stop attacking cell towers and drones and all other technology. Which he did. End of that story. But only Frank and Jenn would ever know that.

The animals in the forests of Montana would remember Aaron, though no humans would ever know that. They would also remember Keerith and Celina, martyrs, lost in a lost cause. Aaron, the ten-year-old who asked, "What can I do?" who grew up to do it all, when he joined with a bear and a sparrow to become BearMann—who lives on. Who is ready to return—if the humans don't keep their promise to keep the planet livable for all its species.

Printed in Great Britain
by Amazon